Carmen
the Cheerleading
Fairy

For Luke and Lucy, my reasons to cheer

Special thanks to Shannon Penney

Copyright © 2017 by Rainbow Magic Limited.

All rights reserved. Published by Scholastic Inc., *Publishers since 1920.* SCHOLASTIC and associated logos are trademarks and/or registered trademarks of Scholastic Inc. RAINBOW MAGIC is a trademark of Rainbow Magic Limited. Reg. U.S. Patent & Trademark Office and other countries. HIT and the HIT logo are trademarks of HIT Entertainment Limited.

The publisher does not have any control over and does not assume any responsibility for author or third-party websites or their content.

This book is a work of fiction. Names, characters, places, and incidents are either the product of the author's imagination or are used fictitiously, and any resemblance to actual persons, living or dead, business establishments, events, or locales is entirely coincidental.

ISBN 978-1-338-05484-2

10 9 8 7 6 5 4 3 2 1   17 18 19 20 21

Printed in the U.S.A.   40
First edition, May 2017

Carmen
the Cheerleading
Fairy

by Daisy Meadows

SCHOLASTIC INC.

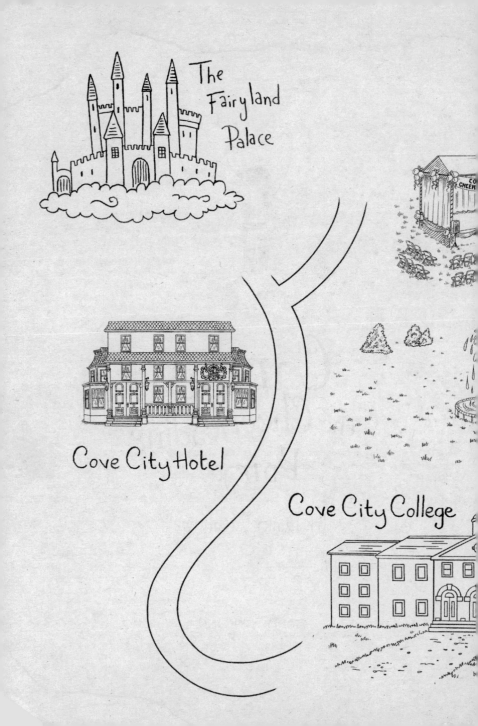

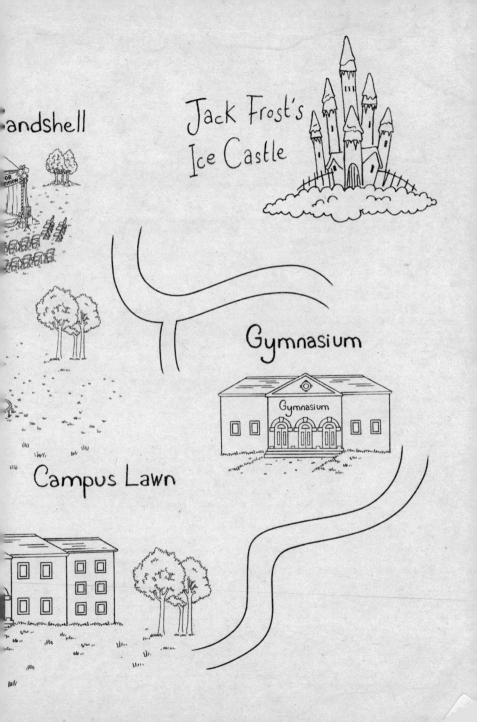

You might think that you have a reason to cheer
But I'll make your good feelings—poof!—disappear.
Magic pom-pom, hair bow, and megaphone, too—
They're mine now! No cheerleading magic for you.

I'm sick of the cheer, the sunshine and smiles.
I have to admit, they're just not my style.
So go on and try all your flips and your tumbles,
But now, thanks to me, you're going to stumble!

**Find the hidden letters in the stars throughout this book.
Unscramble all 6 letters to spell a special cheerleading word!**

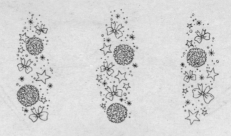

Pom-pom Problems

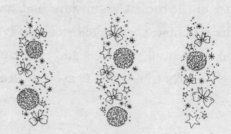

Contents

Perilous Practice   1

A Magic Mission   11

Terrific Tumblers!   21

Cheerleading Chaos!   29

A Reason to Cheer   37

Perilous Practice

"I can't believe we're finally here!"
Kirsty Tate cried, grinning. "I've always
dreamed about taking part in a real
cheerleading competition."

Her best friend, Rachel Walker,
squeezed her hand. "I can believe it! You

and your squad have worked really hard. I'm so glad I got to come along to watch you compete!"

The girls linked arms and skipped across the huge lawn in the middle of the Cove College campus. They'd come to Cove City with Kirsty's parents for the big Junior Cheerleading Competition that weekend! It was Kirsty's first year on a squad, and this was their very first

competition. Rachel and Kirsty had only just arrived, but the weekend already felt magical!

"Tumble over that way!" Mr. Tate called from behind the girls, pointing to a large brick building on one corner of the lawn. The archway over the door read COVE COLLEGE GYMNASIUM.

Kirsty smiled and did a series of cartwheels on her way to the gym. Rachel whooped and applauded as Mr. and Mrs. Tate caught up with them.

"Is the rest of your squad meeting you here?" Rachel asked, pulling the gym door open.

"Yup! It's our last practice before the competition tomorrow," Kirsty said, peering around the massive gym in awe.

"Though I'm not sure how I'll ever find them. This place is huge!"

Girls and boys were scattered all over the gym. Some were stretching and warming up, while others chatted excitedly. Colorful mats covered the floor, and Rachel and Kirsty could see piles of pom-poms and stacks of megaphones over by the bleachers.

"Kirsty!" a voice suddenly called. A girl with a curly black ponytail ran up and gave Kirsty a hug. "Can you believe all this?"

Kirsty shook her head, smiling. "I guess we need a big gym to hold this much cheer!" She turned to Rachel. "Rachel, this is my friend Sunny. She's the captain of our squad."

"I can't wait to see your routine!" Rachel said, waving as Kirsty and Sunny ran off to join their teammates.

"Come on, Rachel," Mrs. Tate said. "Let's find a spot on the bleachers to watch them practice."

From the bleachers, Rachel, Mr. Tate, and Mrs. Tate had a perfect view of the whole gym. There was an awful lot to see! Rachel counted ten different squads

practicing
before she
turned her
attention
back to
Kirsty's
team.
"Okay,
let's go!"
Sunny
cried. She
and a boy
with spiky brown hair led the squad in
their opening cheer. Rachel couldn't
help noticing that they were all out of
sync—some of the kids were forgetting
the words, and others were doing the
wrong arm movements.

Maybe they just need a minute to get warmed up, Rachel thought, frowning.

Kirsty and her friends started to look more and more frustrated as they worked their way through the routine. Things weren't getting better! One girl fell during a simple jump, and another accidentally kicked one of her teammates in the face while doing a cartwheel! Their coach, Mrs. Gold, stood to one side, shaking her head in confusion.

"I've never seen them make so many mistakes," Mrs. Tate murmured. "What could be going on?"

"I don't know," Mr. Tate said. "But they're not the only ones . . ."

He was right! Rachel had been so busy watching Kirsty's squad that she hadn't noticed, but all around the gym, kids were tripping and slipping through their routines. Everyone was forgetting moves, stumbling during tumbles, and dropping pom-poms. What a mess!

Rachel looked back at Kirsty's squad just in time to see them form a pyramid. *Whew,* Rachel thought, watching Sunny climb into place on the very top, *at least that turned out okay!* But suddenly, the

pyramid began to wobble and sway—
and then it collapsed!

Rachel gasped, watching Kirsty
and her teammates topple to the mat.
Luckily, no one seemed to be hurt—but
something was definitely not right . . .

A Magic Mission

Just then, a flash of light caught Rachel's eye. She blinked. What was that?

There it is again! she thought, spotting a twinkle in a nearby pile of pom-poms. She had to get a closer look!

"If it's all right, I thought I'd take a walk around the gym and check out some of the other squads," she said to Mr. and Mrs. Tate.

Kirsty's parents nodded. "Of course, Rachel," Mr. Tate said with a smile. "Just make sure none of those crazy cheerleaders tumble into you!"

Rachel laughed and headed down the bleachers, keeping her eyes on the pile of pom-poms. As she tiptoed closer, she saw the twinkling light again. This time, she could also see what was causing it—a tiny, shimmering fairy, nestled in the pom-poms! She had a dark brown ponytail and wore a colorful cheerleading uniform.

"Hi!" Rachel whispered with a grin, sitting down next to the pile. "I'm

Rachel. Is every–
thing okay?"

The fairy
looked up
at her in
surprise,
and then
she smiled
in relief.
"Oh, Rachel,
I was hoping
you and Kirsty would
find me! I've heard all about you." She
smoothed her skirt and suddenly looked
sad. "I'm Carmen the Cheerleading Fairy.
I'm sorry that I'm not full of more cheer
right now—my magic objects are missing.
Without them, cheerleading everywhere is
a T-O-T-A-L disaster!"

"Let me guess," Rachel said. "Jack Frost is at it again?"

Carmen nodded and crossed her arms angrily. "Of course! He's such an icy old grouch, I shouldn't be surprised that he's taking it out on me."

Rachel glanced around the gym. "So that's why this practice is such a mess!"

"It's awful, isn't it?" Carmen sighed. "These kids have worked so hard to get to this competition, and now nothing is going right.

I'm afraid someone might get seriously hurt if I don't find my magic objects— and fast!"

Nearby, a girl fell to the mat with a hard *thud*. Rachel flinched. Carmen was right—they had to fix this!

"What do your objects look like?" she asked Carmen. "I'll help you find them."

"Oh, thank you!" Carmen cheered, clapping her hands and grinning. "I was looking in this pile of pom-poms, hoping to find my magic pom-pom. It controls athleticism, and helps people nail their moves and cheerleading routines. But I don't see it anywhere!" She shrugged.

"Jack Frost and his goblins never make it easy," Rachel said knowingly.

"I'm also missing my magic hair bow, which controls teamwork— helping people work together and support one another," Carmen said. "And my magic  megaphone is missing, too! That one controls confidence and positive attitudes—helping cheerleaders believe in themselves and look on the bright side."

Suddenly, a loud whistle echoed through the gym. Practice was over! All of the squads—including Kirsty's—looked worried as they gathered their things.

"Here, you can hide in my shirt pocket," Rachel whispered, holding her pocket open while Carmen fluttered in to it. "Let's fill Kirsty in, and then we'll turn that frown upside down!"

Carmen looked up and gave her a halfhearted smile.

Rachel waved to Kirsty, and her friend walked over, hanging her head.

"That was just awful!" Kirsty moaned. "If we perform like that tomorrow, we're going to be the laughingstock of the whole competition."

Rachel gave Kirsty a hug, and then pulled her out of sight behind a rolled-up tumbling mat. "I know you're feeling

down," she said, "but this might cheer you up!"

Carmen peeked out of Rachel's pocket and used her wand to send a swirl of sparkles into the air. "Hi,

Kirsty! I'm Carmen the Cheerleading Fairy."

Kirsty gasped and her face lit up. "Oh, Carmen, I'm so happy to see you!"

Rachel quickly explained the situation.

"So that's why everyone's routines are going so badly!" Kirsty cried. "What a relief."

"Right," Carmen said with a nod, raising her arms above her head. "Gimme an M! Gimme an E! Gimme an S! Gimme another S! What's that spell? MESS!"

Rachel squeezed Kirsty's hand. "If we can find Carmen's magic objects before tomorrow, maybe we can save the competition!"

Kirsty jumped to her feet. "There's no time to lose!" Then she frowned. "But where do we start?"

Terrific Tumblers!

Kirsty, Rachel, and Carmen scanned
the busy gym. There was no sign of
Carmen's magic objects—or naughty
goblins—anywhere!

"We're never going to find anything
in here," Rachel said. "It's too crowded."

Kirsty looked thoughtful. "You're right. Let's look around the hallways until the gym clears out." She flagged down her parents and got permission to explore, and then the girls slipped into the hall. Carmen ducked safely inside Rachel's pocket again.

After being in the loud gym, the hallway seemed extra-quiet. Rachel and Kirsty's footsteps echoed as they walked.

Suddenly, Carmen tugged on Rachel's pocket. "Do you hear that?"

Both girls froze, listening carefully.

Carmen was right! There was something happening up ahead, around a corner. Rachel and Kirsty looked at each other in excitement. Could it be . . . goblins?

Together they raced down the hall, careful to make as little noise as possible. When they reached the corner, they screeched to a stop and peeked around it.

Both girls' jaws dropped! There, in the adjacent hallway, was a whole group of goblins performing elaborate tumbling passes! They did cartwheels, handsprings, and flips, flying through the air as if they had springs on their hands and feet.

"They're amazing!" Kirsty whispered.

Rachel nodded, her eyes wide. "And they never seem to get tired."

It was true! The goblins tumbled over
and over, never stumbling or pausing
for a break. They weren't getting worn
out at all—and they were clearly having
a great time!

Carmen tugged on Rachel's ponytail.
"That's because they have my magic
pom-pom!" she whispered, clapping
her hands in excitement. "Remember,

it controls athleticism—that's why the goblins are nailing so many tumbling passes in a row."

She pointed to a trio of goblins nearby. One of them held a pair of pom-poms while two others tossed him high into

the air . . . and one of the pom-poms was sparkling with fairy magic! "See? There it is!" Carmen continued.

Kirsty almost let out a triumphant cheer, but Rachel clapped a hand over her mouth just in time.

"Sorry," Kirsty whispered with a giggle. "I got a little carried away!"

Rachel grinned. "Let's come up with a plan for getting the pom-pom back *before* the goblins notice us," she said.

Rachel and Kirsty sat down and put their heads together, whispering and thinking hard. But they hadn't gotten very far when Carmen fluttered up out of Rachel's pocket, peeked around the corner, and darted back faster than lightning. She landed on Kirsty's shoulder, looking worried.

"Oh no—we have to go, go, go!" she cried, pointing.

When Kristy and Rachel peeked around the corner again, they understood what Carmen was cheering about. The goblins were still tumbling like cheerleading champions— right through the door at the end of the hallway!

They were heading outside . . . and they were taking Carmen's magic pom-pom with them!

Cheerleading Chaos!

"Don't let them get away!" Carmen cried.

Rachel and Kirsty jumped to their feet and dashed down the hallway after the goblins. Carmen followed Kirsty closely, her ponytail blowing out behind her.

The door was just swinging shut as they reached it and barreled through.

Both girls screeched to a halt as the door slammed behind them. They looked around. Which way had the goblins gone?

"There!" Kirsty cried, pointing to a familiar flash of green disappearing around one side of the gym. "They're heading for the main lawn!"

Rachel followed her friend as fast as she could run, trying to keep her eye on the goblin with the magic pom-pom.

"Good thing the goblins are wearing clothes. Anyone who spots them will probably just think they're kids!"

When they rounded the corner, the girls had no trouble spotting the goblins. The tiny troublemakers were causing quite a scene! They tumbled across the paths, causing students to stumble and bikers to veer onto the grass. They somersaulted through flower beds, leaving a trail of dirty destruction behind them. They even cartwheeled through the fountain at the center of campus, splashing everyone nearby!

"This is chaos!" Kirsty said, shaking her head. "We have to stop them before someone gets hurt."

Carmen tickled Kirsty's ear to get
her attention. "Luckily, it looks like the
goblins are finally ready for a break."

Sure enough, the goblins had flopped
down on the grass, tossing their pom-
poms down beside them. They stretched
out and chatted excitedly.

"Did you see that amazing flip I did in
the fountain?"

"That was nothing compared to my
seventeen back handsprings in a row!"

"I out-tumbled all of you, no contest!"

Rachel rolled her eyes. The goblins
could always find something to brag
about! And that gave her an idea . . .

She whispered her plan to Kirsty
and Carmen. Once Carmen had
tucked herself safely back into Rachel's

shirt pocket, the two girls cheerfully
approached the goblins.

"Wow!" Kirsty exclaimed. "You're all
amazing tumblers!"

The goblins sat up tall, grinning
proudly.

"I wish I could cheer like you," Rachel
added wistfully. "Could you teach us
some moves?"

"Sure!" the goblins cried in unison,
jumping to their
feet.

A goblin
grabbed
the girls'
hands
and led
them to a
wide-open area

of grass. "First, you need to master a back handspring." He demonstrated the move, making it look easy. Then he and his friends spotted Kirsty, then Rachel, making sure they didn't fall as each girl gave it a try.

"Wow, that was fun!" Rachel said with a laugh. She'd never done a back handspring before! And she had to admit—the goblins were good teachers!

"Can you teach us a cheer sequence?" Kirsty asked the goblins.

Another goblin stepped forward.

"Absolutely! Here—you'll need these." He handed each girl a set of pom-poms.

Rachel gasped—and then coughed, trying to cover her surprise. One of the pom-poms in her hand sparkled and shimmered.

She couldn't believe it. The goblin had handed her the magic pom-pom!

A Reason to Cheer

"Ready? Let's go!" the goblin cried, raising his pom-poms into the air.

Rachel waved her pom-poms overhead, winking at Kirsty as the magic pom-pom glittered in the sunlight. She heard a squeal

of excitement from her pocket. Carmen
had spotted the magic pom-pom, too!

The goblin began a cheer sequence,
and his friends scrambled to their feet
to join in. As Rachel lowered her pom-
poms to clap them together, she brought
the magic pom-pom close to her shirt
pocket. Carmen reached out to touch
it, and it immediately shrunk back to
fairy size!

"Got it!"
Carmen
cheered
happily. In
the blink of
an eye, she
twirled up in
the air and
disappeared

in a shower of sparkles—taking the magic pom-pom with her!

Rachel and Kirsty tried their best to pretend that nothing had happened, finishing out the cheer sequence enthusiastically.

When they were done, the goblin who had had the magic pom-pom turned to face them. "Not bad, for beginners," he said. "Of course, you'll need to keep practicing if you want to be as good as me, but that's—"

Suddenly, he froze. He stared at Rachel, who held a pom-pom in one hand and nothing in the other.

"Hey . . . what happened to your other pom-pom?" he asked slowly.

Rachel shrugged. She didn't want to lie, so she chose her words carefully. "I don't

think that pom-pom belonged to you,
anyway—did it?"

The goblin who had showed them
the back handspring stepped forward,
peering around frantically. "Wait! No!
Did you give her the MAGIC pom-pom?"
He smacked his forehead with one big,
green hand. "And now it's missing? Jack

Frost is never going to let us hear the end of this!"

The other goblin snorted. "This never would have happened in the first place if you hadn't been such a show-off!"

"Me?" the first goblin cried. "I'm not the one who handed the magic pom-pom to a total stranger!"

As the other goblins jumped into the argument, hollering and stomping their feet, Rachel and Kirsty slowly backed away unnoticed.

"That was a lucky break," Kirsty said, once they were a safe distance away.

Rachel laughed. "You're telling me! I couldn't believe he handed Carmen's magic pom-pom right to me."

"And now that Carmen's pom-pom has been returned to Fairyland,

our routines should go much more
smoothly." Kirsty sighed with relief.
"I don't think I can handle another
toppling pyramid!"

The girls headed back to the gym to
meet up with Kirsty's parents.

"So what's next?" Rachel asked, linking
arms with her best friend.

Kirsty pulled open the gym door. "Well, it's time to check into the hotel and get dinner with my squad. I can't wait for you to meet everyone! But more importantly . . ."

". . . we have to continue the hunt for Carmen's other missing objects!" Rachel finished.

There was no time to waste. If the girls didn't find Carmen's magic hair bow and megaphone before the morning, Kirsty's first big competition was going to be a big *disaster*!

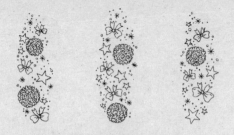

Picture-perfect

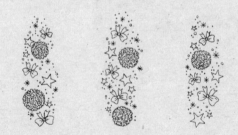

Contents

Teamwork Trouble   49

Hotel Highjinks   59

Goblins Take the Cake   69

Zipping and Zooming   77

Taking a Bow   85

Teamwork Trouble

"Yum!" said Rachel, rubbing her stomach with satisfaction. "That dinner was so good! I hadn't realized how hungry I was."

"Me neither," Kirsty said with a sly smile. She dropped her voice to a whisper. "I guess chasing goblins around all afternoon really helps work up an appetite!"

Rachel laughed. Kirsty was right—running after silly goblins was hard work! As her laugh faded, she glanced around at the rest of Kirsty's squad. They were all walking to the Cove City Hotel after eating dinner together, and there wasn't a smile to be seen! All of the kids looked awfully gloomy . . .

"Here we are," said Mrs. Gold, the squad's coach. She pointed to a large, old, fancy-looking building up ahead. Gaslights flickered on either side of the entrance, and a wrought iron sign over the door read COVE CITY HOTEL.

Even though they were feeling gloomy, the kids on Kirsty's squad couldn't help looking at the hotel in awe.

"Wow," Sunny said. "I can't believe we get to stay here!"

"We'll go grab the bags from our car and check in," Mrs. Tate told Rachel and Kirsty. "Why don't you two have a look around? We'll meet you in the lobby in a little bit."

"Thanks, Mom!" Kirsty said. This was just the opportunity they needed to explore. Maybe they would even track down another one of Carmen the Cheerleading Fairy's missing objects—if they were lucky!

Kirsty turned to the rest of her squad. Everyone was heading inside and up to their rooms. "Good night, everyone. See

you tomorrow
for the big
day!"

The other
kids all tried
to smile and
wave as they
disappeared
through the
front doors.

Kirsty paused outside the hotel
and sighed. "Everyone has been so
snappy and impatient all afternoon.
Our squad usually gets along so well!
At this rate, we won't be working
together very well for tomorrow's
competition." She buried her face in
her hands. "All our hard work could
be for nothing!"

Rachel gave her friend a hug. "This is because Carmen's magic hair bow is still missing," she said. "It controls teamwork, remember? We just have to find it, and then everything will go back to normal!"

Kirsty took a deep breath. "You're right." She stood up tall and squeezed Rachel's hand. "Let's go inside. Hopefully some magic will find us soon—we don't have much time!"

Together the girls pulled open the large front doors of the hotel and stepped into the ornate lobby. A big wooden desk stood off to one side, lit with old lamps and some flickering candles. Huge, overstuffed chairs around the lobby were filled with all kinds of visitors, chatting and relaxing. Jazz music played on

some speakers, and a crystal chandelier glittered overhead.

"This place is amazing!" Rachel said, turning in a slow circle and trying to take it all in.

Kirsty nodded, but didn't say anything. She was too busy studying the crystal chandelier.

Rachel watched her friend curiously. "It's a nice chandelier . . ." she commented after a moment.

"It's not just that," Kirsty whispered. "Look over on the left side. Doesn't it seem . . . *extra*-sparkly?"

Rachel squinted, then gasped. Sure enough, there was a glimmering figure perched

on one arm of the chandelier. "Carmen!"
Rachel cried.

Quick as a flash, the tiny fairy darted
down and ducked into Kirsty's tote.
Fortunately, no one
in the busy lobby
seemed to notice!

Carmen peeked
over the edge
of the bag and
grinned at the
girls. "Hello again!
I hope you're not
too tired from your
long day, because I
can sense my magic
hair bow nearby."

"We were hoping you'd
say that!" Kirsty whispered.

"This old hotel has a lot of nooks and crannies," Rachel said. "The goblins could be anywhere . . ."

"Then we'd better get started!" Carmen cheered.

Hotel Highjinks

Rachel, Kirsty, and Carmen looked around the crowded lobby. There was a lot going on, but they didn't notice anything unusual or goblin-like.

"Let's pick a hallway and start exploring," Kirsty suggested, pointing

to a hall that led off the right side of
the lobby.

Carmen ducked down inside Kirsty's tote
again, and the three friends set off. No
sooner had they left the noisy lobby than
they heard the *ding* of an arriving elevator
up ahead. The doors slid open—and the

girls jumped back! They'd almost been run over by a group of kids leaping and tumbling out of the elevator at full speed!

"Whoa!" Rachel cried. "Those kids are acting crazy!"

Kirsty watched the group somersault down the hallway, frowning. "Those aren't kids . . . they're goblins!"

A tiny gasp came from inside Kirsty's bag. "After them!" Carmen cried.

Rachel and Kirsty raced down the hall as fast as their legs would take them, barely able to keep the tumbling goblins in sight as they went around corners and through doorways.

"Look, one of them is wearing the magic hair bow!" Rachel pointed out, before the goblins ran through a set of swinging doors.

The girls barreled
through the doors
after them—
and then
stopped short.
They'd almost
run right into the
hotel's indoor pool!

"That would have
been a very *unmagical*
surprise," Kirsty
muttered.

On the far side of
the pool, the goblins
were executing perfect cheerleading
tosses and heaving their teammates
into the water. Each goblin landed with
a huge *SPLASH*, soaking the other

swimmers—and all the people on the pool deck, too! The girls watched as the goblin with the hair bow sailed through the air, turning three impressive flips before cannonballing into the deep end.

Kirsty shook her head. "Those goblins are causing so much trouble!"

"That's true, but see how well they're working together?" Carmen pointed out. "That's because they have my magic hair bow." She blinked, squinting at the goblin who had just landed in the water. "Wait—where did it go?"

"There!" Rachel said, pointing to another goblin at the edge of the pool. "They're working together so well that they're also sharing the hair bow—and goblins never share!"

Suddenly, all of the goblins climbed out of the water and ran back through the swinging doors, leaving a slick trail behind them. Rachel and Kirsty followed, trying not to slip!

The goblins sped down the halls again, tossing the hair bow back and forth as they cartwheeled and flipped. When they reached the lobby, they

all began to somersault in unison.
They looked like a row of runaway
bowling balls rolling through the crowd!
People yelped and scattered in every
direction.

"I can't even keep track of which
goblin has the hair bow," Rachel said,
breathing hard as she ran.

"Me, neither," said Kirsty, wiping her forehead. "At this rate, we'll never get it back!"

All at once, the goblins climbed to their feet again and tumbled off down another hallway, clapping and cheering in perfect unison.

"We're green!
We're mean!
We're a top-notch team!
We'll cause more trouble than you've ever seen!"

Carmen peeked out of Kirsty's bag and sighed. "Well, they've got that part right. If we don't stop them soon, they're going to cause a heap of trouble—not just here, but for cheerleaders everywhere!"

Goblins Take the Cake

Rachel and Kirsty skidded around a corner and came to a sudden stop. The goblins had stopped too—and they were standing right in front of the girls! Rachel and Kirsty didn't want to be spotted, so they quickly ducked behind a potted plant. Carmen fluttered silently out of Kirsty's tote and perched on one of the plant's wide leaves.

"What are they doing?" she whispered, peeking at the group of goblins.

Kirsty groaned. "I don't like the looks of this," she said quietly. "Do you see what they're all huddled around?"

"Oh!" Rachel gasped. "It's a . . . wedding cake!"

It was true! The upper tiers of a beautiful white

wedding cake towered above the goblins'
heads. The cake was covered with
frosting flowers, and the girls could see
the small figures of a bride and groom
on the very top. The goblins surrounded
it, giggling gleefully and licking their
lips.

"That's the entrance to the ballroom,"
Kirsty said, pointing to the doors just
beyond the goblins. "And see the sign
over there? 'The Greene and Jones
Wedding.' There's a wedding reception
going on—right now!"

Carmen frowned, crossing her arms.
"This time, the goblins have gone too
far! It's one thing to ruin the
cheerleading competition, but now
they're going to spoil a wedding, too?"
She stomped her foot, and the leaf she

was standing on bobbed up and down. "What a bunch of greedy, green meanies!"

Just then, they heard the goblin with the hair bow speak up. "Okay, team. Here's what we'll do: let's form a goblin pyramid. That way, we can climb up high and snag the delicious top of the cake! That silly bride and groom will never even miss it."

Rachel shook her head in disbelief. "Of course they'll miss it—it's their wedding cake!"

But the other goblins all nodded enthusiastically, cheering, "Great idea!" "Take the cake!" and "Goooo, team!"

They quieted down and listened respectfully as the goblin with the hair bow told them how to form the strongest, sturdiest pyramid. Then they scrambled into position. In no time, they began to form an incredible goblin pyramid right there in the hallway! Five goblins made the base of the pyramid, then four on the next level, three on the next level . . .

Kirsty, Rachel, and Carmen all held their breath as the pyramid grew taller and taller. Before long, it was almost as high as the towering cake! The goblin with the hair bow nodded in

satisfaction, then got
ready to begin
his climb. The
girls could
see that
once he
reached
the top
of the
pyramid, he'd
be able to grab the top tier of the cake
easily!

Suddenly, Kirsty's face lit up. "Team
huddle!" she whispered to Rachel
and Carmen. The little fairy fluttered
down to perch on Kirsty's shoulder,
and Rachel leaned in close. "I have an
idea," Kirsty went on. "But in order for

it to work, we're going to need a little magic ..."

Carmen grinned. "You're in luck, girls!" She held up her wand. "Magic happens to be my specialty."

Zipping and Zooming

Eyes twinkling, Rachel, Kirsty, and Carmen crouched behind the potted plant and watched the goblin pyramid closely.

The girls had to wait for just the right moment to put their plan into action!

The goblin with the hair bow climbed confidently up each level of the pyramid, while his teammates cheered him on.

"You've got this!"

"Nearly there!"

"I can almost taste that cake now . . ."

As the goblin with the hair bow began to climb the uppermost level to take his place at the top, Kirsty gave Carmen a nod. The little fairy took a deep breath. "It's time, girls!"

Carmen waved her wand, and a twinkling of magic surrounded Kirsty and Rachel. In the blink of an eye, they both shrunk down to fairy size! Thin, sparkling wings appeared on each of their backs.

Kirsty fluttered her wings happily. "Being turned into a fairy is the best!"

"You bet it is!" Rachel smiled, flying into the air and giving Carmen a high five. "Now let's take down that pyramid . . . and get Carmen's bow back."

The three fairies darted out of hiding—
and not a moment too soon! The goblin
with the bow had just reached the very
top of the pyramid, and he was about to
reach for the top of
the cake.

"Hey!" Kirsty
cried, zooming
over to the
goblins. "That
cake isn't yours—
and neither is that
bow on your head!"

The goblin with
the bow scoffed.
"Finders keepers!"
His teammates
all laughed and
cheered.

Rachel landed on the goblin's big nose. "That's not how it works. An important part of cheerleading is being a good sport and playing fair."

She stomped her foot, and the goblin yelped, swatting her away with a wave of his hand.

"Get out of here, you pesky fairies!" he grumbled. "We've been working very hard, and we're hungry. If you'll excuse us, now we have some cake to eat." He stretched out a hand toward the top tier of the wedding cake.

But before he could reach the cake, Rachel, Kirsty, and Carmen began flying in circles around his head! They zipped and zoomed, dipped and dove. They couldn't get close enough to grab the magic bow, but they got just close enough to completely confuse and annoy the goblin!

"Stop that! Cut it out!" he cried, waving an arm to shoo them away.

The three friends flew expertly, dodging the goblin's flailing arms. They continued to dart around him like pesky flies—and they couldn't help giggling as he got more and more annoyed!

"I mean it!" the goblin yelled, rising to his knees and swatting at the fairies with

both green hands. He almost sent Kirsty
tumbling through the air with a wild
swing, but she dipped away just in time!
As she did, the goblin lost his balance
and fell to one side, landing on the two
goblins below him with a thud.

"Whoa!" they cried, startled. They
began to wobble, which set off a chain

reaction down the rest of the pyramid. The whole thing started to sway!

Rachel, Kirsty, and Carmen watched from the air as the goblins all desperately tried working together to regain their balance.

"Lean to the left!" one cried.

Another goblin hollered, "Nobody panic! Hold steady!"

But even teamwork magic couldn't save the pyramid. As the fairies looked on, the whole thing tilted, tipped . . . and then came tumbling down!

Taking a Bow

"Ow!"

"Get off me!"

"Whose foot is in my face?!"

The toppled pyramid of goblins lay in a heap, grumbling and groaning. They pushed and shoved while some goblins climbed gingerly to their feet. The rest of the goblins were a tangled pile of arms and legs!

Fluttering in the air above, Kirsty noticed a familiar sparkle. The magic hair bow! The goblin wearing it had been trapped under some of his teammates when he fell. Luckily, his head—and the hair bow—were the only things sticking out of the goblin pileup. This was Kirsty's chance!

Zooming as fast as her wings would carry her, Kirsty made a beeline for the goblin and plucked the bow from his head. Standing on his forehead, she bent over so she could see his face—upside-down!

"Thank you!" she told him sweetly. "The true owner of this magic bow will be very happy to have it back."

The goblin glared at her. His green face turned a furious shade of red . . . but there was nothing he could do! His arms and legs were pinned down by his teammates. The other goblins were so busy arguing and trying to untangle themselves, they didn't even notice that Kirsty was escaping with the hair bow!

"Horrible fairies!" the goblin spat. "Always ruining our fun."

Kirsty grinned and shrugged, then she twirled up into the air with the magic bow in her arms.

Carmen zipped over to meet her. As soon as the little fairy touched her hair bow, it shrunk down to fairy-size. Carmen turned a series of twinkling cartwheels in midair, cheering:

"We've got the bow!

And everyone will know!

Now I have to take it and go, go, go!"

She waved the girls over, and all three
of them landed behind the potted plant
again. With a flick of her wand, Carmen
showered Rachel and Kirsty with fairy
dust. Just like that, they were back to
their regular size!

The three friends watched as the
goblins finally untangled themselves and
got to their feet, rubbing their bumps
and bruises. The rest of the goblins had
realized that the magic hair bow was
gone—and they weren't happy about it!
In fact, they were all so busy arguing that
they completely forgot about the wedding
cake. The whole group of goblins limped
off down the hallway. The girls could
hear them squabbling even after they'd
disappeared around a corner!

"Great teamwork, girls!" Carmen
said with a big smile. "I'm heading
back to Fairyland now, but I'll see you
soon."

Kirsty frowned. "My competition starts
first thing in the morning. I hope we can
find your magic megaphone in time!"

"Don't worry," Rachel assured her. "If
we work together, I have a feeling we

can save the
competition."
Carmen
cheered.
"That's the
spirit!" Then
with a wink and
a wave, she spun
up into the air
and vanished.

Just then, the
girls heard a loud
rumbling. Oh no—what could it be
this time?

Rachel giggled. "I guess all that
goblin-chasing made me hungry . . . that
was my stomach!"

Kirsty linked arms with her best friend.
"I know just the place," she said, leading

the way to the hotel café just off the
lobby.

When they arrived, they were greeted
with waves and friendly hellos—Kirsty's
whole squad was there! They were seated
together in a corner of the café, snacking
and chatting. Kirsty gave Rachel a

relieved smile—it looked like her team was getting along again!

"Carmen's teamwork magic is working again," Kirsty whispered as the friends headed over to join Kirsty's squad.

"Just in time," Rachel said, grabbing a cookie and taking a big bite. "Mmmm . . . magical!"

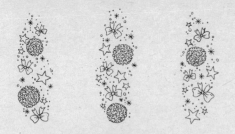

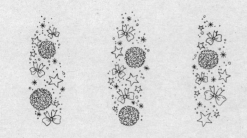

Megaphone Madness

Contents

Goblin Squad   99

A Pep Talk   107

An Icy Emcee   117

Tricks and Tumbles   127

Trophy Time   137

Goblin Squad

"I can't believe the big competition is today," Kirsty said nervously, biting her nails as she climbed onto the shuttle bus. "It seems like we've been practicing forever!"

Rachel followed her friend down the bus aisle and plopped down in a seat next to her. "Your squad has worked so hard," she said with a grin. "You're going to rock this!"

Kirsty gave a tiny smile. Then she sighed and peered down at her sneakers.

"Hey," Rachel said, nudging Kirsty with her shoulder. "What's going on? Are you nervous?"

"Yeah, but it's more than that." Kirsty looked around the bus, frowning. "I know in my head that we're ready to compete, but I don't *feel* ready. And it doesn't seem like anyone else does, either!"

Rachel took in the gloomy faces of Kirsty's teammates. Kirsty was right— not a single kid looked happy or excited! Where was the squad spirit?

Kirsty dropped her voice to a whisper. "What if we don't find Carmen's magic megaphone in time? Then my squad won't be able to find our confidence before the competition."

Rachel hated to see her friend so sad. She threw an arm around Kirsty's shoulders and flashed her a big smile. "Then we'll just have to make sure Carmen gets her megaphone back soon—that's all there is to it!"

By the time the bus pulled up to the Cove College campus, Kirsty was already looking a little more cheerful. She couldn't help grinning as she peeked out the window. The outdoor venue was packed with people! Cheerleaders milled around and warmed up quietly in different brightly colored uniforms, while their families and friends took pictures, handed out snacks, and gave pep talks. Banners and balloons hung all around the outdoor stage, and people were already filing into rows and rows of folding chairs. Upbeat music blared over a set of giant speakers. It was exactly what Kirsty had always dreamed a big cheerleading competition would be like!

Now if only Jack Frost and his goblins don't ruin it for everyone, she thought grimly.

As everyone filed off the bus, Kirsty's teammates began chattering in low voices.

"Wow, the stage is huge!"

"People are already claiming seats!"

"Look—they're even selling T-shirts!"

Rachel and Kirsty climbed down the bus steps and looked around carefully. They knew they were supposed to let

the magic find
them, but
the clock
was ticking!
Maybe
they could
spot a clue
that would
lead them
to Carmen's
megaphone ...

Before they
could even step away from the bus, the
girls heard a booming voice nearby.

"One, two, three, four; you watch us,
you'll want more!"

Rachel raised an eyebrow, and Kirsty
nodded. Together, they walked over to
join a large crowd that had gathered

on the grass. Everyone seemed to be watching a performance, but there were so many people that Rachel and Kirsty had trouble seeing through the crowd!

"Clap your hands, stomp your feet, because our squad can't be beat!"

As the same voice boomed out again, the crowd suddenly parted. The girls had a clear view of the performers jumping, cheering, and clapping energetically.

"They're amazing," Kirsty said under her breath, looking gloomy.

"They're *goblins*!" Rachel whispered with a gasp.

A Pep Talk

Kirsty clapped a hand over her mouth.
"You're right!" she said. "I didn't even
recognize them in those uniforms."

Both girls stifled a giggle. The goblins
were dressed head-to-toe in matching

green cheerleading uniforms, each holding sparkly pom-poms. They even wore green hair bows—even though none of them had any hair!

Rachel glanced around the crowd. "No one seems to notice anything strange about them," she said. In fact, the crowd had started clapping along. The goblins' confident energy was infectious! They added some jumps, tumbling passes, and tosses to their routine, and no one could deny it—they were fantastic.

"Whoa," Kirsty said, grabbing Rachel's arm as the goblins completed a tricky toss.

Rachel sighed. "I know—they're really good."

"No! Well, yes, they are, but that's not all," Kirsty said. She dropped her voice to a whisper and pointed. "That one has Carmen's magic megaphone!"

The goblin whose voice they had heard when they got off the bus was holding a megaphone up to his mouth. When the girls looked closely, they could see that it sparkled with fairy magic!

A shiver ran up Rachel's spine. "We found it! Now we just have to get it away from the goblins before the competition starts."

Just then, the group of kids next to Rachel and Kirsty started talking among themselves.

"We'll never be able to beat THEM," one boy said with a groan, staring at the goblins.

Another girl nodded. "Yeah, we might as well just drop out of the competition now."

Kirsty's eyes grew wide. "We have to get that megaphone back fast," she said to Rachel. "But how? Every-one is watching the goblin squad.

We can't even get close to them. It's hopeless!"

Rachel squeezed her friend's hand. "You only feel that way because the goblins have the megaphone. Everyone's confidence has vanished—mine, too." She shrugged sadly. "I don't know if we can stop them this time, but we still have to try."

"The only thing to do is wait for them to finish performing," Kirsty said.

"Right," Rachel agreed. "Then we'll try to snag the megaphone as fast as we can and get it back to Carmen . . . if we can find her."

Kirsty grinned. "I think I can help with that!" She pointed behind Rachel to a nearby fountain. The water near the top of the fountain twinkled and shimmered.

It almost looked like a reflection of the sunlight, but when the girls squinted, they could see a familiar tiny figure perched on the edge.

"Carmen!" Rachel cried, rushing over to the fountain with Kirsty on her heels.

The little fairy grinned up at them, kicking her feet in the trickling water. "Hi, girls! I was hoping you'd find me. There are so many people here!"

"People . . . and goblins," Kirsty said, raising an eyebrow.

As the girls told Carmen all about the goblin squad, the fairy's face grew pink. She crossed her arms and huffed, "They have some nerve!" Then she looked closely at Rachel and Kirsty, who both stood with slumped shoulders. "You seem a little down in the dumps, girls."

Rachel shrugged. "I just don't see how we're going to get your megaphone back in time, Carmen."

Carmen twirled up into the air in a burst of sparkles, then zoomed down and landed on Rachel's shoulder as quick as a wink. "Lucky for you both, I'm great at pep talks! Listen, you're only feeling like this because my megaphone isn't in Fairyland, where it should be." She fluttered her wings against Rachel's neck, and Rachel giggled.

"But you two have proven over and over that you can do anything you set your minds to!"

Kirsty and Rachel had to smile. Carmen was right!

"It's time to stop those goblins—and save the competition!" Kirsty cheered.

Carmen laughed. "Now that's the spirit!"

An Icy Emcee

Luckily, the goblins finished their performance, and the crowd headed off to find their seats.

Carmen tugged on Rachel's hair and pointed. "Follow those goblins!"

With some pep in her step, Rachel started after the green troublemakers—but Kirsty grabbed her arm. "Wait!" she whispered, pointing to the competition stage. "This may be even trickier than we thought . . ."

Just then, the sun disappeared behind a cloud. Rachel, Kirsty, and Carmen all shivered as a tall, thin figure stepped out onto the stage, holding a megaphone up to his mouth.

"Welcome! Welcome, everyone, to the Junior Cheerleading Competition!" a familiar voice bellowed through the megaphone.

"Oh!" Rachel cried in surprise, clapping a hand over her mouth. "It's Jack Frost!"

Kirsty nodded grimly. "And he has Carmen's magic megaphone now."

118

Without hesitating, Carmen darted into the air. "Why, that horrible, icy grouch! I'm going to give him a piece of my mi—"

But before Carmen could go anywhere, Rachel gently grabbed her foot between two fingers and held her back. "Careful, Carmen. You can't let the crowd spot you!"

Carmen sighed, her wings drooping as she slumped down on top of Rachel's head. "You're right. I just can't stand seeing that wicked thief with my megaphone, especially now that the competition is about to start!"

Up on stage, Jack Frost was still chatting up the crowd, waving his arms and smiling widely. "You're going to see some amazing cheerleading today, folks!"

"Yeah, from your cheating goblins," Kirsty mumbled under her breath.

"So let's get this competition started!" Jack Frost continued. Then, to the girls'

surprise, he began stomping his feet in rhythm—and launched into a cheer of his own!

"We're so glad you all are here,
Let's fill this stage with tons of cheer!
1, 2, 3, 4,
The squad that wins will have the highest score!"

With that, the crowd burst into applause. Jack Frost bounced excitedly on his toes as he waved the magic megaphone over his head.

"Now if the competing squads will all assemble backstage, we'll get started in just a few minutes," Jack Frost went on after the applause died down. "Enjoy!" Waving to the crowd, he ran offstage.

Carmen looked at the girls with wide eyes. "Well, that was . . . strange."

"You said it," Rachel agreed. "I've never seen Jack Frost so cheerful!"

Kirsty frowned. "Your magic megaphone must be really powerful, Carmen. It's not safe with Jack Frost!"

The girls raced around to the back of the stage, with Carmen out of sight on Rachel's shoulder. But they didn't get very far before . . .

BAM!

Rachel and Kirsty both ran smack into Jack Frost himself!

"Watch it!" he snapped icily. Fortunately, he barely even glanced down at them! Instead, he tossed the magic megaphone to one of the nearby goblins. "You're up first," he called to the goblin squad. "You'd better win that trophy—it's going to be the centerpiece of the trophy case in my Ice Castle."

The girls ducked behind a set of stairs leading up to the stage. They had to think fast!

"Hey, look!" Rachel said, pointing to where the goblin squad was gathered. "There, on the ground. Don't those look like—"

"Extra uniforms!" Kirsty cried, peering at the green clothing scattered among the goblins' messy bags.

Carmen frowned, confused. "But what good are those going to do us?"

"I have a crazy idea," Rachel said with a grin. "And it just might work . . ."

Tricks and Tumbles

With no time to waste, Rachel and Kirsty
darted out, grabbed two of the extra goblin
uniforms, and ducked back behind the
stairs. They quickly changed into the green
outfits, including pom-poms. When they
finished, both girls turned to face Carmen.

"So?" Kirsty asked the little fairy.
Carmen
winked.
"You're the
best-looking
goblin
cheerleaders I've
ever seen! Now go
get 'em!" She pointed
to where the goblin squad was gathering.
They were about to take the stage!

Rachel squeezed Kirsty's hand, then
took a deep breath. Together, the two
friends joined the group of goblins,
elbowing and jostling along with the
others in order to fit in.

"Look," Kirsty whispered as they
all climbed onstage. "That goblin

leading the way has Carmen's magic megaphone!"

Rachel nodded, feeling more confident now that the megaphone was so close by. "Don't let him out of your sight!"

The girls stepped onto the stage, following the goblins' lead as they jumped around excitedly, rousing the crowd. Everyone in the audience clapped and cheered as the goblins took their places.

Rachel and Kirsty stood near the back of the stage. They copied the goblins' movements as the leader's voice boomed through the magic megaphone.

"We're green, we're mean, we're a top-notch team!"

The routine went on, and the girls followed along. All the while, they kept an eye on Carmen, who sat on the rafters above the stage. Suddenly, the little fairy waved her wand and sent a tiny stream of sparkles into the air. That was their cue!

Before the goblins knew what was happening, Kirsty was doing a perfect tumbling pass across the stage. She turned a series of cartwheels and handsprings until she reached the goblin with the megaphone—then she snatched it right out of his hand as she tumbled by!

Without hesitating, Kirsty held the megaphone to her mouth and started a cheer.

"We've got spirit, yes we do! We've got spirit, how about you?"

The goblins all froze, looking at one another in confusion. Just then, Rachel stepped to the front of the stage and began cheering along with Kirsty, waving her pom-poms in the air. The goblins shrugged and followed along, trying to act like they knew what was going on— exactly as the girls had hoped they would!

Kirsty continued cheering, and Rachel gathered a group of goblins to set up a basket toss. They quickly got into formation. When Kirsty was done with her cheer, the goblins lifted her up and tossed her into the air!

As Kirsty sailed up into the air, a flash of light flickered overhead—Carmen! The tiny fairy darted to Kirsty and grabbed the magic megaphone from her hand. As soon as she touched it, the

megaphone shrunk back down to its
Fairyland size! Carmen squealed with
delight and fluttered away before anyone
could spot her.

The goblins easily caught Kirsty and set her back down on the stage. No one even seemed to notice that she no longer had the megaphone! They worked their way through the rest of the routine, and finished to a huge round of applause from the audience.

Grinning from big ear to big ear, the goblins ran off the stage, with Rachel and Kirsty trailing behind them.

Jack Frost was waiting at the bottom of the stage steps, scowling. "Not bad, not bad," he said. "Now give me that megaphone for safekeeping."

The goblins all looked around at one another, holding up empty hands.

"I don't have it!"

"I thought YOU had it!"

"Who had it last?"

"Um, it wasn't me ..."

Rachel and Kirsty stood back, watching carefully as the goblins scrambled to cover up their mistake.

But Jack Frost wasn't amused. "You fools!" he thundered. "Do you mean to tell me you LOST the magic megaphone?"

Trophy Time

Kirsty and Rachel froze in their tracks.
They looked at each other with wide eyes.

"We can't let Jack Frost punish the
goblins for this," Rachel whispered.

Kirsty paused thoughtfully. "You're right, that wouldn't be fair. Plus, if he gets really angry, he could ruin the competition with his ice magic anyway—even though Carmen has her magic objects back!"

Rachel stood up tall. She felt more confident than she had all weekend, now that the magic megaphone was back in Fairyland! "There's only one thing to do."

With that, the girls stepped forward. "Excuse me, Jack Frost?" Kirsty called.

Jack Frost's spiky head whipped around to look at the girls, and his mouth curved into a sneer. "What could you pesky girls possibly want?"

"We want to explain what happened to the magic megaphone,"

Rachel said calmly. "It's been
returned to Fairyland by Carmen the
Cheerleading Fairy."

Jack Frost's icy eyebrows shot up.
"What?!" he spat. "I'll get back at
that horrible fairy for this, mark my
words!"

"No, you won't," Kirsty said, with her hands on her hips. "The megaphone wasn't yours. Neither were the magic pom-poms or the magic hair bow. It's not right to take things that don't belong to you!"

A frustrated yowl came from Jack Frost's mouth, and he raised his wand. The goblins all cowered in fear. Rachel and Kirsty looked at each other in panic. Now what?

But before Jack Frost could summon any wicked ice bolts, a sparkling light zoomed right in front of his face. A little fairy landed on his hand—Carmen!

"Stop!" she cried. "I have an idea that I think you'll like, Mr. Frost."

Shaking with rage, Jack Frost narrowed his eyes. "I should send you tumbling off

my hand right now," he said to Carmen.
"But I have to admit, I'm curious. Tell
me your idea—and it had better be
good!"

Carmen fluttered up into the air. "Even
better—I'll show you!"

She zipped off, and returned a second later with a huge gold trophy floating over her head! She held her wand in the air, using her fairy magic to move the giant trophy along, since it was much too big for her to carry. Then she set the trophy down on the corner of the stage, and flew down to perch on top of it.

"I know you wanted a trophy for the case in your Ice Castle," she said. "But rather than hijacking the cheerleading trophy, I thought you might like this one better. I made it just for you!"

Jack Frost walked around the trophy slowly, examining it from every angle. Rachel and Kirsty couldn't help smiling as they watched him. The top of the huge trophy was shaped just like his spiky head!

After a few moments, Jack Frost's face broke into a sudden grin. "I love it!" he cried, lifting the trophy up over his head triumphantly. "I can't wait to add it to my trophy case." He turned to the goblins. "Come on, team—2, 4, 6, 8, time to go, my castle awaits!" With a blast of icy air, he and the goblins disappeared.

Carmen cartwheeled through the air, clapping her hands. "We did it, girls!

Now the rest of the competition can go on as planned!"

Kirsty glanced at her watch. "Speaking of which, I need to get out of this goblin uniform and into my own uniform—my squad is up next!" She gave Rachel and Carmen each a high five.

"Go get 'em, Kirsty!" Rachel cheered, as her friend ran off.

Carmen held up her wand and shot a rainbow of magical sparkles into the air. "I have a feeling the rest of this competition is going to be truly magical!"

RAINBOW
magic
THE Friendship FAIRIES

Rachel and Kirsty have found all of
Carmen's missing magic items.
Now it's time for them to help

Esther
the Kindness Fairy!

Join their next adventure in this
special sneak peek . . .

The Start of Summer

"It's so amazing to be back on Rainspell Island again—*together!*" said Kirsty Tate, leaning out her window and taking a deep breath of sea air.

Her best friend, Rachel Walker, clapped her hands and bounced up and down on her tiptoes.

"Today is the start of the most amazing summer vacation *ever*," she said. "I'm sure of it!"

They were sharing a room at the Sunny Days Bed & Breakfast on the island where they had first met and become best friends. They were so happy to be there again on vacation together. The girls shared a quick hug before rushing down the narrow stairs to the cozy breakfast room. Their parents were already there, poring over leaflets about activities on the island.

"I'm sure we can find some new things to do," said Mr. Walker, "even though we have visited this island so many times before."

"How about a nice long hike?" suggested Mr. Tate as the girls slipped into their seats and poured some cereal.

"It'd be interesting to explore more of the island—we all love seeing its beautiful plants and trees."

Rachel and Kirsty shared a smile. They had an extra-special secret reason why they loved Rainspell Island so much. It was here that they had first become friends with the fairies!

"Hiking would be a great start to the trip," said Mr. Walker. "Let's head out after breakfast, shall we?"

"Here's something interesting," said Mrs. Walker, holding out a bright yellow flyer. "It's called the Summer Friends Camp."

Rachel took the flyer and read out loud. "'A day camp for children staying on the island. Make new friends and join in lots of fun activities.' It sounds awesome!"

As Kirsty and Rachel were looking
at the flyer and chattering about the
activities, the breakfast-room door
opened and Mr. Holliday came in.
He ran the bed and breakfast, and he
glanced at the flyer as he put some toast
down on the table.

"My daughter Ginny's helping run
that camp with her best friend, Jen," he
said.

Kirsty and Rachel exchanged a special
smile, wondering if Ginny and Jen's
friendship was as strong as theirs. They
knew that they were lucky to have each
other.

"Is it OK if we go to the Summer
Friends Camp instead of going on the
hike?" Kirsty asked. "It sounds like lots
of fun."

"Of course," said Mr. Tate. "We'll see you later. You can tell us all about it!"

"The Summer Friends Camp is held at Rainspell Park," said Mr. Holliday. "I'm sure you'll have a wonderful time."

When they had finished breakfast, the Tates and the Walkers put on their backpacks and hiking boots and set out on their hike. Rachel and Kirsty waved good-bye and then headed off toward Rainspell Park. The bed and breakfast was on a tree-lined road that overlooked the ocean, and as they walked along they saw the ferry heading toward the island.

"Remember when we met on the ferry that first day?" Rachel asked, smiling at her best friend. "That was one of the best days of my life."

"Mine, too," said Kirsty. "Everything I do is more fun now that I have you to share it with—including our fairy adventures!"

The girls held hands and smiled when they saw that they were both wearing the friendship bracelets that Florence the Friendship Fairy had given them. Rainspell Island was the place where the girls had first made friends with the fairies, so it had a very special place in their hearts.

"I hope we'll meet some more fairies while we're here," said Rachel. "I love making new fairy friends."

"Fingers crossed we'll make some new human friends, too," Kirsty added. "The Summer Friends Camp sounds like such a fun idea."

They reached the entrance to Rainspell Park and walked through the open gates, gazing around at colorful flowerbeds and huge old trees. The wide gravel paths were dotted with benches, and a large fountain was bubbling and splashing beside the bandstand.

"Look," said Rachel, "there's a sign for the camp."

A bright yellow sign pointed them past the fountain and around a bend. They saw a large tepee-style tent in the middle of the grass. It was surrounded by colorful balloons, and the sign next to the tent said, *Welcome to the Summer Friends Camp*!

Still holding hands, Rachel and Kirsty walked into the tent. It was cool inside, and decorated with rainbow-colored silk.

A smiling teenage girl hurried to greet them. She was wearing a mint-green name tag that said, *Jen*, decorated with delicate, dark-gray birds.

"Welcome to our camp," she said. "Come and join us!"

A Surprise in the Goal

Peering over Jen's shoulder, Rachel and Kirsty could see another teenage girl standing at a craft table with eight other children. Jen led them over to the table and the other teenager smiled at them.

"Hi, girls, it's great to see you here! I'm Ginny. Right now we're all making name tags. It'd be great if everyone could introduce themselves."

The children smiled at Rachel and Kirsty and went around the table introducing themselves. Then two children named Lara and Oscar made space for the girls to join them.

"Have some markers," said Oscar, moving a cup of markers over so they could both share it.

"I have enough stickers for all of us," added Lara, placing her sticker sheet between them all.

"Thanks, that's so kind of you," said Rachel with a smile.

They both took a blank name tag and started the fun of decorating.

"So is this your first time on the island?" Jen asked Rachel.

"No, we've been here lots of times," said Rachel. "It's actually where Kirsty and I first met and became best friends, so it's a really special place for us."

"You're so lucky," said Lara, as she carefully drew a butterfly on her name tag. "I've been here for three days and I love it. I wish I lived here!"

"It's definitely a great place for friendship," said Ginny, exchanging a smile with Jen.

"Everyone is so nice," Kirsty whispered to Rachel. "I'm really glad we came."

As soon as the name tags were finished and the craft table was cleaned up, Ginny asked everyone to come outside.

"We have two outdoor activities planned for today," she said. "First we'll play a game of soccer, and then Jen and I will challenge you all to a water-balloon fight!"

"Let's split into teams," said Jen. "I can't wait to get started!"

She divided the group into two, and Rachel and Kirsty found themselves on different teams. They grinned at each other—everyone was so friendly that they didn't mind being separated at all!

"All we need now are some goalposts," said Ginny. "Does anyone have anything we can use to mark where the goal is?"

Rachel pulled off her bright pink hoodie and three of the other children also donated colorful sweatshirts and cardigans. Then the positions were assigned and the game began. Kirsty was the goalie for her team, and she stood in the goal with her knees bent and her heart thumping as Rachel's team brought the ball closer and closer to her. She felt nervous because she didn't play soccer very often and she didn't want to let anyone down.

Lara darted across the field and kicked the ball as hard as she could. The ball flew toward Kirsty, who dived sideways, hands outstretched. She felt it brush her fingertips, but she couldn't quite reach it, and the first goal had been scored.

"GOAL!" yelled Rachel, jumping up and down in delight.

RAINBOW magic™

Which Magical Fairies Have You Met?

- ❑ The Rainbow Fairies
- ❑ The Weather Fairies
- ❑ The Jewel Fairies
- ❑ The Pet Fairies
- ❑ The Sports Fairies
- ❑ The Ocean Fairies
- ❑ The Princess Fairies
- ❑ The Superstar Fairies
- ❑ The Fashion Fairies
- ❑ The Sugar & Spice Fairies
- ❑ The Earth Fairies
- ❑ The Magical Crafts Fairies
- ❑ The Baby Animal Rescue Fairies
- ❑ The Fairy Tale Fairies
- ❑ The School Day Fairies

Find all of your favorite fairy friends at
scholastic.com/rainbowmagic

HiT entertainment

RMFAIRY15

RAINBOW magic™

SPECIAL EDITION

Which Magical Fairies Have You Met?

- ❏ Joy the Summer Vacation Fairy
- ❏ Holly the Christmas Fairy
- ❏ Kylie the Carnival Fairy
- ❏ Stella the Star Fairy
- ❏ Shannon the Ocean Fairy
- ❏ Trixie the Halloween Fairy
- ❏ Gabriella the Snow Kingdom Fairy
- ❏ Juliet the Valentine Fairy
- ❏ Mia the Bridesmaid Fairy
- ❏ Flora the Dress-Up Fairy
- ❏ Paige the Christmas Play Fairy
- ❏ Emma the Easter Fairy
- ❏ Cara the Camp Fairy
- ❏ Destiny the Rock Star Fairy
- ❏ Belle the Birthday Fairy
- ❏ Olympia the Games Fairy
- ❏ Selena the Sleepover Fairy

- ❏ Cheryl the Christmas Tree Fairy
- ❏ Florence the Friendship Fairy
- ❏ Lindsay the Luck Fairy
- ❏ Brianna the Tooth Fairy
- ❏ Autumn the Falling Leaves Fairy
- ❏ Keira the Movie Star Fairy
- ❏ Addison the April Fool's Day Fairy
- ❏ Bailey the Babysitter Fairy
- ❏ Natalie the Christmas Stocking Fairy
- ❏ Lila and Myla the Twins Fairies
- ❏ Chelsea the Congratulations Fairy
- ❏ Carly the School Fairy
- ❏ Angelica the Angel Fairy
- ❏ Blossom the Flower Girl Fairy
- ❏ Skyler the Fireworks Fairy
- ❏ Giselle the Christmas Ballet Fairy
- ❏ Alicia the Snow Queen Fairy

SCHOLASTIC

Find all of your favorite fairy friends at
scholastic.com/rainbowmagic

3 stories in each one!

HIT entertainment

RMSPECIAL20

RAINBOW magic™

Magical fun for everyone! Learn fairy secrets, send friendship notes, and more!

HiT entertainment

www.scholastic.com/rainbowmagic

RMACTIV4